Quentin Blake

Three Little Monkeys

ILLUSTRATED BY
Emma Chichester Clark

HarperCollins *Children's Books*

First published in hardback in Great Britain by HarperCollins *Children's Books* in 2016
First published in paperback in 2017
This edition published in 2018

1 3 5 7 9 10 8 6 4 2

ISBN: 978-0-00-816448-5

HarperCollins *Children's Books* is a division of HarperCollins *Publishers* Ltd.

Text copyright © Quentin Blake 2016
Illustrations copyright © Emma Chichester Clark 2016

Visit our website at: www.harpercollins.co.uk

Printed in China

MIX
Paper from
responsible sources
FSC™ C007454

FSC
www.fsc.org

This book is produced from independently certified FSC™ paper
to ensure responsible forest management.

For more information visit: www.harpercollins.co.uk/green

Hilda Snibbs came into the hall
and closed the door.

"I'm home!" she called.
"Where are you?"

Now, some people have dogs, and some people
have cats, but Hilda Snibbs—

Hilda Snibbs had
three little monkeys.

Their names were Tim
and Sam and Lulu.

Hilda fed them on slices of carrot and apple
and banana and worried about their health.
They were very lively.

One morning Hilda took her shopping basket and went to buy some bananas.

"Be good while I'm away," she said.

When she had gone Tim and Sam and Lulu soon felt bored,

so they crept into the hall cupboard to see what they could find to play with.

They threw everything into the hall.

They tried to open the umbrellas.

They climbed into the Wellington boots.

They pulled the laces out of the shoes.

And they pulled all the feathers out of Hilda's best hat.

When Hilda came home she found the most dreadful mess.
There were feathers all over the place.
And her poor hat!

"I'm really very disappointed in such naughty little monkeys," she said.

Tim and Sam and Lulu looked at her
with their big round eyes and said nothing.

The next day Hilda went out to buy
a new hat.

"Make sure you are good while
I'm away," she said.

When she had gone the three little
monkeys soon began to feel bored,

so they went into the sitting room
to see what they could find to play with.

They emptied the wastepaper basket.

They tore up
the newspapers.

They tipped over
the flower vase.

Then they found Hilda's
knitting and they clambered
over the furniture with it until
it was tied in knots.

When Hilda came home and went into the sitting room she found the most awful mess. There were flowers all over the place.

And her poor knitting!

She clutched it to her and wailed, "What have I done to deserve these wretched little monkeys?"

Tim and Sam and Lulu looked at her with their big round eyes and said nothing.

The next day Hilda took her shopping basket
and went out to buy some more wool.

"And **remember** to be good while
I'm away," she said.

When she had gone the three little
monkeys soon began to feel bored,

so they went into the kitchen to see
what they could find to play with.

They pulled all the
scrubbing brushes
out of the cupboard.

They emptied the
cleaning powder
on the floor.

They got into the pedal bin and threw
out all the potato peelings. And they
tipped a saucepan of soup all over
the kitchen floor.

When Hilda came home she found the most appalling mess. There were brushes and potato peelings all over the floor.

And her soup!

Hilda banged the saucepan on top of the stove and shouted, "Great grief! How long can I put up with these dreadful little monkeys?"

Tim and Sam and Lulu looked at her with their big round eyes and said nothing.

The next morning Hilda took her basket and went out to buy a tin of soup.

"And be **absolutely sure** that you are good while I'm away," she said.

When she had gone the three little monkeys soon began to feel bored,

so they crept up the stairs and into the bathroom to see what they could find to play with.

They unrolled all the toilet paper.

They squeezed the toothpaste.

They nibbled the soap
and didn't like it.

And they poured Hilda's
favourite shampoo
into the basin.

When Hilda came home she went up to the bathroom to wash her hands. She found the most unbelievable mess. There was toilet paper and water and soapsuds all over the floor.

And her poor shampoo!

Hilda gave a screech. She tore her hair
and rolled her eyes.

"Oh," she cried.
"Oh, for a peaceful life without
these **wicked little monkeys!**"

The next day Hilda had to go and see her mother,
who was in bed with a bad cold.

"And don't forget you must, must
be very good while I'm away!"

It was late in the evening
when Hilda came home.
She looked round the hall.
Everything was neat and tidy.

But where were the three
little monkeys?

She looked into the sitting room.
There was her knitting on the chair and the newspaper was
in a neat pile: but Tim and Sam and Lulu were nowhere to
be seen.

"What can have become of them?" Hilda said to herself.

She went into the kitchen.

Everything was clean and shining and in its proper place:
but there was no sign of the three little monkeys.

"Oh dear," said Hilda. "This is very worrying.
What can have happened to them?"

She went upstairs to the bathroom.

Everything was clean and shining
and in its proper place:

but there was no sign at all
of the three little monkeys.

"This is dreadful," said Hilda, and she gave way to despair. The tears rolled down her cheeks. She tried to dab them with her handkerchief, but there were still lots that dripped onto the floor.

Soon her handkerchief was soaking wet.
She went to the cupboard to get a dry one.

And there were Tim
and Sam and Lulu.

They looked at her with
their big round eyes and
said nothing.

That night Hilda went up the stairs
to bed with a happy heart.

And as she slid between the sheets she discovered
all the spoons and forks from the kitchen
and three tins of sardines in tomato sauce.

But that is the sort of thing you have to expect
if you have three little monkeys.